Wordsworth Dances the Waltz

To the memory of my mother, Matsue Kakugawa, who loved to dance the waltz and fox-trot at PTA meetings at Kapoho School when we were students—and who continued to dance in her imaginative mind long after she was diagnosed with Alzheimer's disease.

Frances H. Kakugawa

For Emily Burt

Melissa DeSica

Text © 2007 Frances H. Kakugawa

Illustrations © 2007 Melissa DeSica

ISBN 978-0-9790647-3-9

LIBRARY OF CONGRESS CONTROL NUMBER: 2007924418

Printed in Korea

Design
Leo Gonzalez

Production
Maggie Fujino

Activities, discussion questions and other features available in the Wordsworth Readers Guides, available online at www.bookshawaii.net

WATERMARK PUBLISHING
1088 Bishop Street, Suite 310
Honolulu, HI 96813
Telephone: Toll-free 1-866-900-BOOK
Web site: www.bookshawaii.net
email: sales@bookshawaii.net

Wordsworth Dances the Waltz

Story by
Frances H. Kakugawa

Illustrations by
Melissa DeSica

WATERMARK
PUBLISHING

Thank you...

To Red Slider for the Rubber Band game and for helping edit this story. To Meghan Laughlin for inviting me as her grandma to Noelani School's Grandparents' Day. To George Engebretson and Duane Kurisu of Watermark Publishing for letting Wordsworth support their commitment to promote the literary arts to young readers. And last, but by no means least, to all the readers who asked for more Wordsworth stories, thank you.

Frances H. Kakugawa

Dear Readers,

Thank you for all the letters you sent me after reading my first book, *Wordsworth the Poet*. I have saved all your letters. I hope you will write to me again at the address below. I hope to meet you again in my third storybook.

Aloha,

Wordsworth

Wordsworth the Poet
Watermark Publishing
1088 Bishop St., Ste. 310
Honolulu, HI 96813
wordsworth@bookshawaii.net

Poor Wordsworth was puzzled. He couldn't understand why there was so much whispering around the house since Grandma had come to live with them. He remembered Grandma's last visit a year ago. She was full of life then, talking all the time and dancing. Oh, how she loved to dance! If there wasn't anyone to dance with, she danced by herself. If there wasn't any music, she danced without it. And if she happened to see Wordsworth watching, she would grab him and twirl him around until he forgot how silly he felt. Then Wordsworth and Grandma would laugh and laugh as they danced around the room.

But now Grandma stayed in the guest room of their house, which was nestled in a rainforest in the Hawaiian Islands. Wordsworth shared the house with his mother, father, three brothers and sister.

But these days, instead of music, he more often heard the frequent whispering of his parents. A stillness had fallen over their home as though it were always three o'clock in the morning. His brothers and sister were told to walk softly and to keep their voices down so they wouldn't disturb Grandma. He felt like the entire house was holding a big secret.

Wordsworth was a poet. Writing poems always helped him make sense of things. So he wrote a poem about all the whispering.

Shhhhh

Hush, hush,
Grandma's losing her memory.
Hush, hush,
She's forgetting
To flush the john.
Hush, hush,
She's lost her glasses again.
Hush, hush,
She's forgotten my name.
Hush, hush,
Shhhhh.

His house was so quiet—like a library or a hospital—that
Wordsworth began spending more time with his friends.
For almost a year now he and his best friend, Emily, had been
taking karate lessons with their classmates Eliot and Dylan.
They all loved practicing this Japanese art of self-defense that taught
them how to use quick, sharp blows with their hands and feet.
Emily had already earned a blue belt and Eliot and Dylan had their
yellow belts, but Wordsworth was still stuck back at the first level,
trying to get beyond the beginner's white belt. But as his *sensei*,
or teacher, said, "We are all special in our own way." So it
didn't bother Wordsworth that his belt was still white or that
Dylan teasingly called him "White Belt Wordsworth."

One Saturday morning, Wordsworth put on his *gi,* the white robe worn by karate students, and went to meet Emily. As they walked to the karate *dojo,* or school, Wordsworth and Emily passed an elderly mouse sitting in a wheelchair under a tree, with his caregiver standing nearby. When the old mouse saw Wordsworth and Emily in their uniforms, he raised his hands with a weak "Hah!" as if to make a karate chop. Wordsworth and Emily looked at each other and, without a word, assumed the stance of the *kata,* a set of karate movements. Sometimes good friends know exactly what the other is thinking without saying anything.

After performing the last movement in the kata, they stood and bowed to the old mouse, who now had a big smile on his face. Wordsworth and Emily smiled back, then scampered off to the dojo.

Wordsworth wondered what the old mouse thought when he saw children running and playing. Did he wish he was young again? Was he sad because he could no longer run or practice karate?

But no! The old mouse had seemed delighted as he watched them perform their kata. Hmmm, Wordsworth wondered, is that how it is for Grandma, too? Is she happy just watching children run and play? Wouldn't she enjoy hearing a little noise and laughter, too?

So Wordsworth, being a poet, put his thoughts down on paper. This time, he compared an elderly person to a *bonsai*, a tree or shrub that has been dwarfed by artistic pruning. He knew that it took many years to cultivate a bonsai into a beautiful shape.

Bonsai

Knees knotted.
Veins frozen.
Legs rooted.
Arms perfected.
Years of toil
Plugged within.
His aged form
Sits serene.
Winds and rains
Beat on down
Only to quench
His thirsty tongue.
He sits bent

In silent thoughts,
While all around,
Are sprouting young
Tossing and stretching
Their willowy arms.
He listens in silence
To all their laughter,
Their dreams, their hopes.
He watches in silence,
Their youthful limbs
Dancing, dancing
Without a care
In the breeze.

Are his thoughts
Dancing too,
From where he sits?

Late the next day, while Wordsworth and Emily and Eliot and Dylan were sitting at the beach, they played a game called Rubber Band, in which they made up stories about things they saw in nature. Dylan had given it that name because the game always stretched the imagination. Wordsworth's friends, who knew that he was a poet, often tried to see things as he did. Now the sun was setting, and the clouds over the distant mountains were beginning to look like melted crayons. Eliot, the mouse with the crinkly whiskers, began the game. "I see a flying fish with blue, pink and rose fins and a silver-blue tail! Oh, look at him fly, like a trapeze artist, with his fins all stretched out."

"And look, now there's
a dragon following the fish!"
Emily added. "Look at the fire
flashing out of its mouth like a
volcano with lava spurting out.
Oh, just look at that enormous
head with the dark eye sockets
and that long, long tail of
purple and orange scales!"
"Uh oh!" Dylan shouted.
"He's two inches away from the
flying fish. He's going to have a fish fry.
What say you, poet Wordsworth?"

But Wordsworth was silent, lost in his own thoughts,
riding on the flying fish, carried to places of his imagination.
Through a forest of trees all fiery crimson and golden, in a
kaleidoscope of colors brighter than any rainbow in the skies.
Over a mountain to a palace beyond, where no one ever
grew old. A place where birthdays were never celebrated.
"Wordsworth! Hel-*lo*! Where are you? Do you think
the dragon's out to eat the fish? Wordsworth?"
Jolted back from his thoughts, Wordsworth laughed
and said, "No, the dragon is escorting the fish
home to his palace beyond the mountain."
Eliot stood and bowed, proclaiming in a haughty voice,
"Of course! My fish is no ordinary fish! He's royalty!
His Highness, the Flying Fish!"

The four friends sat and watched the animals in the sky as the winds slowly changed the colors and shapes. The sun began to sink behind the mountains. Emily said quietly, "Look. The dragon lost his head and tail. Now he looks like a friendly gray dog escorting his master, the flying fish."

"The fish is losing its sharp flying fins, too," Eliot said, "Now it looks like a long gray snake." Soon everything melted down into gray candles as the sun sank lower and lower behind the mountains. Wordsworth stood up. "Well," he said, "The royal parade has pulled up stakes and is moving on to the next town." "Time for us to go too." Emily said. "It's dinnertime."

On their walk home, Emily picked up a dry leaf and gave it to Wordsworth. Dylan, who loved to tease, said, "Uh oh! I'll bet Wordsworth's going to write another poem."

Dylan was right. That night Wordsworth thought of how things and people were always changing, like clouds shifting their shapes and colors. He thought of his grandma not being the grandma he knew a year ago. That elderly mouse in the park was no longer the strong young mouse he had once been. Change was all around him. "Some changes are good, aren't they?" Wordsworth asked himself as he looked at the leaf Emily had given him. He marveled at how an old dry leaf could still be beautiful, like delicate lace or a butterfly wing. Then he sat down and wrote a poem to give to Emily in the morning.

A Gift from Emily
a dried, brittle leaf
covers my palm,
such delicate lace,
butterfly wings,
…like memories…
…of what once was….

The next Monday was Grandparents Day at school. All grandparents were invited to a special lunch and program. The cafeteria was filled with the students and their grandmas and grandpas. Children who didn't have grandparents invited their neighbors or elderly family friends. All except Wordsworth. His Grandma was home in her room.

His father had said, "No, Grandma can't go to school with you on Monday. It's time you should know, Wordsworth—Grandma is losing her memory. This happens to some people when they get older. If she goes to Grandparents Day, she won't understand what's going on, so it's best to keep her home."

That morning, before going down to breakfast, Wordsworth had gone into Grandma's room, where she was still asleep. Sitting next to her bed, he had written a poem about what his father had told him. He remembered the days when he was a younger mouse, when Grandma would hug him so tight he could hardly breathe.

Grandma

When Grandma hugged me
And said, "How's my Wordsworth?"

When Grandma sent me presents
On special days of the year,

When Grandma gave me candy
Right before dinnertime,

When Grandma told me stories
Way past my bedtime,

She was Grandma to me
Because she was Grandma,

Not because she had a memory
Or because she knew my name.

Now that she's losing her memory,
She's still my Grandma, isn't she?

Wordsworth had put his new poem down on Grandma's bed and watched her sleep. Suddenly he'd realized he was going to be late for school. He'd jumped up and scampered from the room, forgetting all about the poem lying on the bed. But was it his imagination or had he seen a faint smile on Grandma's face as he rushed out the door?

Now, at the Grandparents Day festivities, Wordsworth was getting ready to recite a poem he had written especially for the occasion. As he stood up on stage, he looked up to see his parents walk into the cafeteria. Between them walked Grandma, wearing her best party dress. She even had a fresh flower in her hair. Wordsworth's heart was beating like hummingbird wings. He waited until they were all seated. Then he began.

Grandparents

You are like that trunk of an oak
Whose roots grow deep into our soil
Sending branches up to the skies.

You are a book without end,
Filled with stories and folklore
Of when you were a child
Long before we were born.

You are a treasure
On our treasure hunt,
Gold, trinkets and gems
Where X marks the spot.

Grandparents,
Your stories, your memories,
We will preserve and treasure
For our children and their children.

Grandparents,
We honor you
On this day.

Everyone applauded at the end of the poem, and no one clapped louder than Grandma. "We're so proud of you," his mother told him. "I found your poem on Grandma's bed this morning. It reminded me that she is still a big part of this family, and I realized how much she would want to be here today."

When Wordsworth arrived home after school, he found Grandma sitting in the living room listening to a CD. He recognized the tune— "The Blue Danube Waltz" by Johann Strauss. He saw that she was moving her feet in time to the music, so he took her hands and said, "Grandma, remember how you used to dance the waltz? Come, dance with me." He turned the volume up.
Grandma smiled and stood.

She was a little wobbly on her feet but he held her tightly and soon they were moving slowly to the 1-2-3 rhythm of the waltz. Her body and head moved to the music of "The Blue Danube." A smile played on her face. Her eyes looked as if she were remembering something from long ago.

The Dance

Come waltz with me,
In your dancing shoes
1 2 3
1 2 3
She hears the music
To his dance,
1 2 3
1 2 3

She follows his lead,
The dance begins,
1 2 3
1 2 3

Swish and swirl
Around we go,
1 2 3
1 2 3

Wordsworth's parents stood in the doorway, surprise and delight showing on their faces. "The Blue Danube" had ended and another Strauss waltz, "The Artist's Life," began playing. Wordsworth saw his father bow to his mother and offer her his hand, and then they were waltzing right along with Wordsworth and Grandma. 1-2-3, 1-2-3.

The room was filled with music and laughter,
just like it used to be. Wordsworth's brothers and sister
heard the music and laughter and joined in, clapping 1-2-3
in time to the music, and then started to waltz themselves.
Their neighbors heard the commotion and came to the door,
and soon they were dancing too. And in the middle of it
all was Grandma, the happiest mouse in the room.
Wordsworth looked at her and asked himself, "Will Grandma
remember this in the morning?" He didn't know and he really
didn't care. She was happy in the moment, dancing.
And that was all that mattered.

After that day, Grandma was no longer kept in her bedroom. She now joined the family when they played cards, watched movies, or went out to dinner or to the mall. And yes, she continued to dance. The whispering in the house stopped and there was noise and laughter once again.

She wasn't the same Grandma of a year ago, of course. Her memory continued to fade, and Wordsworth now knew that she would probably lose more than her memory, too. Someday, she might not recognize him anymore. She might need someone to help her eat and, like the old mouse in the park, she might need a wheelchair.

But she was still his Grandma. And nothing could ever change that.

1 2 3
Come dance with me
1 2 3
1 2 3...

The End